For my mom, and my grandma
(whom we also called "Mom" . . . it's a long story!)

BLOOMSBURY CHILDREN'S BOOKS
Bloomsbury Publishing Inc., part of Bloomsbury Publishing Plc
1385 Broadway, New York, NY 10018

BLOOMSBURY, BLOOMSBURY CHILDREN'S BOOKS, and the Diana logo are trademarks of Bloomsbury Publishing Plc

First published in the United States of America in February 2024
by Bloomsbury Children's Books

Text and illustrations copyright © 2024 by Anu Chouhan

Bloomsbury books may be purchased for business or promotional use. For information on bulk
purchases please contact Macmillan Corporate and Premium Sales Department at
specialmarkets@macmillan.com

Library of Congress Cataloging-in-Publication Data
available upon request
ISBN 978-1-5476-1104-1 (hardcover) • ISBN 978-1-5476-1105-8 (e-book) • ISBN 978-1-5476-1106-5 (e-PDF)

Art created digitally
Typeset in Delima MT Std
Book design by Yelena Safronova
Printed in China by Leo Paper Products, Heshan, Guangdong
2 4 6 8 10 9 7 5 3 1

To find out more about our authors and books visit www.bloomsbury.com and sign up for our newsletters.

Hair Oil Magic

Anu Chouhan

BLOOMSBURY
CHILDREN'S BOOKS
NEW YORK   LONDON   OXFORD   NEW DELHI   SYDNEY

For Meenu Kaur, Sunday was better known as "Magic Hair Day."

Mommy would begin by swirling sweet-smelling oils together in a bowl.

Meenu loved to watch. It always looked like
Mommy was mixing up a magical potion.

Then, Meenu would nestle into Mommy's lap as she
gently massaged her potion onto Meenu's scalp.

Two tidy braids kept Meenu's hair out
of her face as she played in the yard . . .

. . . and helped Biji prepare lunch,
while also letting the oil absorb into
each strand.

At bath time, Mommy washed Meenu's hair with a special shampoo.

Meenu loved how bouncy and sparkly her wavy locks looked at the end of the day!

But Meenu thought the best part about Magic
Hair Day was the fuzzy, magical feeling she got
when the oil was massaged into her hair.

It was like little floating stars

twinkling around her heart!

For this week's Magic Hair Day, Meenu wanted
to show Mommy and Biji that she could use the
magic oils without any help.
She found the shelves loaded with bottles of oil.

Meenu took a deep breath and recalled what
Mommy told her about mixing oils.

Fenugreek oil for silky soft hair,

while rosemary grows it long.

Castor oil helps roots repair,

and coconut makes it strong!

Meenu carefully dropped some fenugreek oil into her mixing bowl.

Sniff sniff · · · That's not it!

Then, she poured in a bit of castor oil and mixed it with her finger.

Squish squish . . . Would that work?

Meenu plopped some of her magic potion on her head and rubbed it around. But the fuzziness and magic just weren't there.

"Maybe I need to add more."

One by one, Meenu added a little bit of each oil to her bowl. She mixed and mixed, then rubbed and scrubbed all over her hair.

"I still don't feel any magic," Meenu grumbled.

What was she missing?

Then, Meenu noticed a glimmering purple glass bottle on the top shelf.

"That *has* to be the magic key! Mommy always adds a few drops of oil from that bottle to all her potions!

Meenu got up on a stool and stretched as far as she could until she finally grabbed the bottle. But all that oil on her hands caused it to slip way up into the air!

"Are you okay, Meenu?"

"I wanted to show you both I was ready to use magic hair oil, but I just can't do it."
Meenu sobbed. "I'm so sorry."

Meenu sniffled as Mommy helped
her into the bathtub and began to
softly massage Meenu's head.

"There's that fuzzy, magical feeling
again!" Meenu gasped. "How did you
do that without any magic oil?"

Biji smiled. "The magic isn't in the oil itself. It's created from the moments we share together on Magic Hair Days.

That fuzzy, magical feeling
is your mommy's love!"

Mommy nodded. "Biji used
to massage oil into my hair too.

Her mother did the same for her,
and so did her mother's mother."

"The magic is in the ritual that has been passed down for generations!

"This way, we learn to take care of our hair, and then pass that knowledge on when we're all grown up."

After her bath, Meenu gave Mommy her own Magic Hair Day.

As Meenu carefully combed oil through Mommy's silky black hair, she could feel the stars around her heart return, and she knew

Mommy could feel them too.

Author's Note

The ritual of hair oiling between parents and their children in South Asian families is one steeped in tradition and bonding, and has been an important part of hair care for thousands of years.

I was born in Canada, but my mom's family immigrated here from Punjab, India, while she was still a teen. When I was little, my mom would oil my hair once a week—just like Meenu and her mommy! It was a familiar comfort that I looked forward to. My grandma would also tell me about the benefits and uses of many traditional ingredients like fenugreek, cloves, and amla, which she learned about while growing up in Punjab. Like many other first-generation South Asian kids, my hair oiling became a routine over time, which has helped me to maintain the habit now as an adult.

Meenu's Magic Hair Day Tips

✦ If you'd like to try out hair oiling, your parents or guardian should check with a doctor to see if you are allergic to any types of foods used to create oils. If you have itchy flakes on your scalp (called dandruff), it would be better to get that treated before applying oil.

✦ Brush out your hair before applying any oil to avoid tangles and knots, and to allow it to evenly cover your hair.

✦ Don't tie your hair too tight after oiling! Tie or braid it gently, or wear a loose shower cap to avoid pulling or breaking your hair.

✦ Certain hair types respond better to certain oils. For example, thick and coarse hair might benefit from a rich oil like coconut or castor. However, that might be too heavy for thinner hair! Something light like argan oil would be better.

✦ It's fun to make hair potions with oils you might already have around the house. But learn from Meenu's mistake . . . be sure to ask your parents or guardian for help to avoid making a sticky mess!

✦ Remember, anyone can benefit from having a Magic Hair Day!